Real Heroes Read!

realheroesread.com

HEROES A2Z

#9: Ivy League All-Stars

David Anthony
and
Charles David Clasman

Illustrations
Lys Blakeslee

Traverse City, MI

Home of the Heroes

abigail

andrew

zoë

CHAPTER 1:
MEET THE HEROES

Welcome to Traverse City, Michigan, population 18,000. The city has everything you might expect: malls, movie theaters, schools, and playgrounds. Kids swim here in the summer and build snowmen during the winter. Sometimes they pretend that they live in an ordinary place.

But Traverse City is far from ordinary. It is set on one of the Great Lakes and attracts tourists in every season. Thousands of people visit every year. Still, few of them know the city's real secret. Even fewer talk about it. You see, Traverse City is home to three incredible superheroes. This story is about them.

Meet Abigail, the oldest of our heroes by a whole eight minutes. When it comes to sports, she can't be beat—not at iceskating, not at interceptions on the football field, and certainly not at the Ironman competition. She has also been known to strike out the side in a baseball game with just one pitch.

Andrew comes next. He's Abigail's twin brother, younger by a measly eight minutes. If it has wheels, Andrew can ride it. He's impressive, imposing, and inspiring on wheels. In fact, he can round the bases like nobody else. Get it—round, like a wheel? First base, second base, third base, home! Another inside-the-park homerun leaves the infielders out.

Last but definitely not least is Baby Zoë. She's proof that big things can come in small packages. She still wears a diaper, but she can fire a sunflower seed all the way to the baseball Hall of Fame in Cooperstown, New York. Watch out, Babe Ruth! Zoë puts the *it* in *spit*.

Together these three heroes keep the streets and neighborhoods of Traverse City, Michigan, and America safe. Together they are …

CHAPTER 2:
SINGING SALMON

"Impossible!" Zoë grumbled, tossing up her arms in frustration. Strike ninety-nine! Who had ever heard of such a thing?

On the pitcher's mound, Abigail frowned. "It's not *that* bad," she said. "Remember, practice makes perfect."

Zoë scowled. Ninety-nine pitches had resulted in ninety-nine strikes. Not one hit. Just *whiff, whiff, whiff!* She was done practicing for the day.

To prove it, she raised her baseball bat in both hands and snapped it in half over her knee.

Crack!

"Whoa!" Andrew exclaimed. "Hit the brakes, Zoë. Don't get so wound up."

"Yeah," Abigail agreed. "You're still a superhero. No other baby can lift the Mackinac Bridge or pull Santa's sleigh."*

They were right, of course, but Zoë didn't want cheering up. She wanted to feel sorry for herself.

"Inconsolable," she muttered, turning her back. She couldn't use the Mackinac Bridge as a baseball bat. She had never hit a homerun on Christmas Eve.

*See Heroes A²Z #2: Bowling Over Halloween
and Heroes A²Z #8: Holiday Holdup

"All aboard!"

A sudden call from Manager Mom cut across the ball field. It was time to get on the bus.

Andrew and Abigail celebrated by throwing their gloves into the air. "Comerica Park, here we come!"

The heroes were going to Detroit. Tomorrow they would play in the Little League championship game. The game would take place at Comerica Park, where the Detroit Tigers played. Their team, the Traverse City Salmon, would play against the Garden City Sprouts.

Make that two teams plus nine innings plus hundreds of fans. The sum? One winner and one loser.

Still, when Andrew saw the bus, he forgot all about baseball. The oversized wheels won his attention.

"I'll drive!" he shouted, dashing up the bus's steps.

Driver Dad stopped him at the top. "I'll handle it," he told his son. "Why don't you sit in back with your teammates?"

He wanted Andrew to focus on the upcoming game. But mostly he wanted to keep the bus on the ground. Andrew had a habit of treating wheels like wings whenever he drove.

Andrew shrugged. No big deal. He was all about wheels. He knew he would get another chance to drive soon.

"Who wants to sing campfire songs?" he asked. Teammates high-fived him as he strolled to a seat in the back of the bus. Good thinking!

So for the new few hours, Andrew and his teammates sang songs. The ride from Traverse City to Detroit gave them plenty of time to sing all their favorites.

"Itsy!" Zoë suggested first. She loved the one about the spider that climbed up the water spout.

Next came *Bingo, Old McDonald,* and *Do Your Ears Hang Low?* But everyone's ultimate favorite was *Take Me Out to the Ballgame*, a baseball classic.

CHAPTER 3:
JACOB THE JUGGLER

The team sang until Driver Dad pulled into the hotel parking lot in Detroit. Then everyone got quiet. The big game wasn't until tomorrow, but it seemed very close and real now.

"Hey, there's J.J.!" Andrew shouted, breaking the silence. He pointed excitedly out the window.

Outside the hotel's front door stood a boy. His name was Jacob, but most everyone called him J.J. He was the heroes' cousin, and, like them, he was a superhero.

J.J. was the same age as Abigail and Andrew, and he played shortstop for the Garden City Sprouts. More importantly, he never dropped the ball. Not once. Not ever.

His superpower wouldn't let him. He was Jacob the Juggler, J.J. for short. He had been juggling since the day he was born.

As he grew, J.J. kept juggling and kept improving. When he was in preschool, his teachers had to keep a close eye on him at all times. If they didn't, J.J. would snatch his younger classmates and juggle them. Talk about rock-a-bye baby!

Even now, J.J. rarely stopped juggling. He was the best shortstop in Little League history because of it. No ball got past him. No catch was out of reach. He was like a human octopus with a glove on every tentacle.

Any hit to his side of the field was an automatic out. Just ask his teammates. They had to practice against him. Without J.J., they would not have made it to the championship game.

So when the bus finally stopped, the heroes galloped off to greet their cousin. They weren't surprised to see him juggling. Five suitcases spun in the air above his head.

"Hey, family!" he said, not slowing for even a second.

Instead, the heroes slowed. J.J. had changed. His normally brown hair was full of ivy leaves, and his skin was as green as a leprechaun's hat!

CHAPTER 4:
DOC BOT

"You're green!" Andrew and Abigail gasped at their cousin.

"Illness?" Zoë asked in concern.

J.J. shook his head. "Doc Bot has all the Garden City players on a strict diet. We eat vegetables for breakfast, lunch, and dinner. Guess what we get for a bedtime snack?"

The heroes shrugged together.

"Vegetables!" J.J. chuckled, answering his own question. "You didn't expect me to say pistachio pudding, did you?"

Vegetables. That explained it. The greenish skin and leafy hair were probably side effects from the all-veggie diet. They would fade after the baseball season. So that left only one question.

"Who's Doc Bot?" Abigail asked.

"Our new coach," J.J. answered. "Doctor Botany. Did you know that botany is the study of plants? Cool nickname, huh? Doc Bot."

Zoë marveled at her talented cousin. He made sense of everything.

"Intelligent," she said.

"Jacob was always a smart boy," Manager Mom said as she stepped off the bus.

Driver Dad agreed. "He takes after his uncle," he said. "Smart runs in the family."

For a brief moment, Abigail wondered about that. Using her sporty superpower, she could outrun anyone. Did that mean she could outrun smart, too?

"Why don't you kids hit the pool?" Driver Dad suggested. "Manager Mom and I will check into the hotel."

Zoom! A second later, the adults were alone. The heroes, their teammates, and cousin J.J. were all proceeding to the pool.

"Last one there can't outrun a brain!" Abigail called over her shoulder. Not that anyone had an idea of what she was talking about. But that didn't matter. Abigail reached the pool first. She won the race, same as always.

She also won a game of water polo against her teammates. Against all of them. Eight versus one. She might have let them score a point, if they had put up a better fight.

No one got mad though. That was just how it went. Abigail couldn't be beat at sports. She was a superhero.

Not that that stopped Andrew from getting even. In a pool, a water polo ball was as good as a wheel.

Take that, Abigail, you showoff.

Splash!

The fun, however, ended abruptly. The Garden City Sprouts and their coach, Doc Bot, arrived.

"Get out of the water, Salmon," Doc Bot snapped. "My little saplings need a turn in the pool."

Saplings? The Garden City coach was taking the veggie theme very seriously. He was calling his players plants! What kind of baseball coach was he?

CHAPTER 5:
THAT BABY

Later that night, Zoë slept badly. She tossed and turned, stuck in a nightmare. A cactus monster invaded her dreams. It chased her up a chimney. It pursued her onto the porch. It hunted her down hallways everywhere she hid.

No matter how fast Zoë flew, the monster's prickly arms were inches away. *Look out, Zoë! Fly!*

Finally the monster caught her. Its scratchy
limbs wrapped around her in an unfriendly hug.
Prickers poked her pink pajamas.

Zoë's eyes popped open and she shrieked.

"Itchy!" she wailed, sitting straight up in bed
like the Frankenstein monster come to life.

Slowly the nightmare faded and Zoë forgot about it. Abigail and Andrew stood over her crib. The pair was dressed in their baseball uniforms.

"We're itchy, all right," Andrew grinned down at her. "Itching to play ball."

Abigail smacked her right fist into the baseball mitt on her left hand. "Batter up, Zoë. It's time to go."

Play ball? Batter up? That's right! Today was the championship game! Zoë would show her siblings that she was a slugger. Better yet, she would do so in baseball style.

First she led off by swinging into action, right over the bars of her crib. Second, she slid into the bathroom at a run. A walk just wasn't in her rotation. Third, she hit cleanup with a double play—face washed and teeth brushed, always fair and never foul. Then she knocked it all home by stealing safely out the door in a line-drive shot. She left her siblings standing at the plate, just like after a third strike call. Zoë 1, Twins 0.

In fact, she beat everyone to the bus and claimed the backseat for herself.

Andrew scowled when he arrived. Foul ball, Zoë! That seat was his. But he plopped down next to their friend Rabbit.

"How's it rolling?" he asked.

Rabbit stammered nervously. "G-Garden City hopped easily over the c-competition. I hope we d-don't get b-bounced."

Andrew blinked. *Hopped? Bounced?* Did Rabbit think they were bunnies?

"Whoa!" Andrew said, raising both hands. "Slow down. Our team will cruise to victory."

Behind him, Zoë disagreed. She cleared her throat and wagged a finger. "Illogical," she said.

In other words, don't count your chickens before they hatch. The game could go either way. Either team could win. Andrew shouldn't be overconfident, but Rabbit shouldn't worry either.

Her advice seemed to calm both boys. At least, that is, until Mo leaned over from across the aisle. Mo was the leader of the baseball team's marching band. He also liked to tease Zoë.

"Did that baby learn to bat yet?" he asked Andrew. He never used Zoë's name. He always called her "that baby."

Today his joke was about batting. Last time it was about Zoë's drumming.*

*See Heroes A²Z #7: Guitar Rocket Star

"Insufferable," Zoë wanted to say. Sometimes Mo was too much. But Driver Dad's voice cut her off.

"Attention, sports fans!" he announced over the loudspeaker. "Grab your gloves, snatch your sneakers, and claim your caps. It's time to play baseball. Next stop, Comerica Park!"

A moment later the bus stopped, and everyone went silent. They had arrived. The Little League championship game was about to begin.

CHAPTER 6:
THE DREAD ZEPPELIN

Chattering excitedly, the players bounded off the bus and proceeded into the park. Into Comerica Park. Today they didn't need tickets. They were going to play baseball where the Detroit Tigers played. How awesome was that?

When they reached the field, a shadow passed over them. Zoë pointed into the sky. "Inflated," she said.

Everyone looked up. A chubby green blimp floated overhead. It was as long as their team bus and shaped like a watermelon. The words *Dread Zeppelin* were printed on its side.

"Do you think it has wheels?" Andrew wondered out loud. He had never ridden in or driven a blimp before. Did it even have a steering wheel?

Abigail slugged his shoulder. "Got me," she said. "But your mouth has a motor. Now be quiet. Something is happening."

Suddenly the blimp's windows flew open, and kids started climbing out. They fearlessly grabbed vines that dangled from the blimp and slid down like firemen on poles in the stationhouse.

As they descended, the kids became clearer to everyone on the ground. They were members of the Garden City Sprouts baseball team. Team captain J.J. led the way.

"I could do better," Abigail snorted. She had, too, last Halloween.*

*See Heroes A²Z #2: Bowling Over Halloween

What an entrance! The crowd in the stands cheered. If the Sprouts could score runs for style, they had already won the game.

But they weren't finished yet. When they hit the ground, the Sprouts quickly spread out. Then they started gardening. Yes, gardening. Not warming up or going over a game plan. They used shovels and trowels to dig and plant. The second baseman sewed seeds, the pitcher planted perennials, and the outfielders fertilized flowers. Soon Comerica Park looked like a blooming garden ready for harvest.

Rabbit's sister Princess made a face. "Eww! Those other kids are digging in the dirt. A princess would never do that."

Sinister laughter caused her and the heroes to turn around. Doc Bot grinned wolfishly at them. In his hand he clutched a cucumber-shaped device with buttons on it like a TV remote control.

"Digging in the dirt?" he repeated with a sneer. "My blossoms will leave you in the dirt. Six feet under, that is. Prepare to be planted!"

Before anyone could respond, Doc Bot pushed a button on his cucumber-shaped remote control. Thunk! Metal clunked loudly overhead.

"Something's coming out!" Princess exclaimed, pointing at the blimp.

Two doors fell open on the bottom of the blimp. There was a large compartment inside it. A gigantic watering can descended from within and slowly started to tip.

"Looks like rain!" Andrew howled. "Run! Go!"

It looked like rain, all right, but it wasn't. Not on this sunny summer day. The liquid that spilled out of the watering can was green and smelled like chemicals.

"Invigorate?" Zoë wondered, thinking of the new plants all around her.

Was Doc Bot trying to fertilize the field? Was this to make his team's plants grow? He was the strangest baseball coach the heroes had ever seen. What else did he have planned for today?

CHAPTER 7:
SCRATCH THREE, YOU'RE OUT

Green liquid fell like rain out of the giant watering can that hung from the bottom of the blimp. The heroes and their teammates covered their heads with their gloves and dashed into the dugout.

"Immersed," Zoë complained, meaning she was soaking wet. In fact, all of her teammates were dripping as they huddled around Manager Mom.

Manager Mom dripped, too. She also twitched. She wanted to give the team a pep talk, but she just couldn't concentrate.

"My back!" she finally exploded. "It itches! So do my arms and legs. *Please scratch!*"

Driver Dad grinned. "The itching explains your twitching," he snickered. Then he, too, started to twitch. "Oh, no! It's happening to me now!"

Just like that, the twitching and itching spread throughout the dugout. Soon the whole team caught it.

Abigail threw down her mitt, and the rest of the team copied her. "We can't scratch with those on our hands!" they wailed.

But no gloves meant no game. Had the Traverse City team already lost?

"Batter up!" the umpire announced. It was time to find out.

Andrew batted first and swung on the first pitch. He itched too much to wait longer. He had to scratch, and fast.

Crack! He smacked a shot toward J.J., and the race was on. Andrew dropped his bat. J.J. snatched the ball and threw.

"Out!" shouted the umpire.

The ball arrived at first base long before Andrew. That was because he had stopped to scratch his itchy feet.

"I've got flat tires," he muttered. Talk about burning rubber!

Zoë batted next. Like Andrew, she itched uncontrollably, but Zoë never hit the ball anyway. She whiffed every time. Her superpowers hadn't helped her master the art of batting yet.

So strike one went the first pitch. *Whoosh* and a miss. Strike two went the second. *Whoosh* again. Strike three went the third. Some surprise.

"Yer outta here!" bawled the umpire.

Zoë shuffled back to the dugout with tears in her eyes.

Feeling confident, Rabbit hopped to the plate. He was used to twitching. His nose always twitched. Why else would he be nicknamed Rabbit?

Still, today was worse. He twitched and itched everywhere. So much so that he started scratching his back with his bat.

Tap! A pitch rapped his bat and dribbled to the ground.

"Run!" Manager Mom cried. A hit was a hit, no matter how weak. But Rabbit just kept scratching. He didn't realize he had hit the ball until he was out.

So much for the Salmon's first at bat. Three outs meant it was time to switch sides.

CHAPTER 8:
ITCHY INNING

Manager Mom tried to rally her team between bouts of scratching. "Let's go, Salmon," she cheered. "Play defense out there. We aren't swimming upstream yet."

Now there was an idea. Swimming. A quick dip would probably cure everyone's itching problem.

Too bad there wasn't a pool or lake nearby. Comerica Park offered a lot of cool attractions—a carousel, fireworks, thirteen-foot statues of famous Tigers, and even a Ferris wheel. Just nowhere to swim. Even the giant watering can had retracted back into the blimp.

The disappearance of the watering can was a relief. It meant no more green rain. But the Salmon players continued to itch. Not even Abigail could concentrate totally on baseball.

"I can't stop scratching!" she grumbled on the pitcher's mound.

"Well, this batter can't hit," Rabbit replied. He played catcher. "He can't even see. He doesn't eat carrots." Even itchy, Rabbit thought about bunny food.

Abigail scowled and wound up. It was time to play ball. Then—*whoops!*—she loaded the bases on twelve straight wild pitches. That put batters safe on first, second, and third bases with nobody out.

J.J. batted next, number four in the line-up. He marched confidently to the plate and stared at Abigail without blinking. Using his bat, he pointed over the centerfield fence.

"That's where I'm going to hit it," he said. "A homer for this hero."

The gesture surprised Abigail. It wasn't like J.J. He had never bragged before, not even the time he had juggled black bears and saved the Boy Scouts.

Today J.J. didn't only brag. He backed up his words with action.

Smack! He whacked Abigail's first pitch deep, deep into the outfield. Back, back, back it blazed.

Normally Zoë would catch such a ball. No problem, she could fly. But today she was busy and not paying attention. She was sitting in the grass and scratching herself like a dog with fleas. The ball soared over her head and over the centerfield fence.

SPROUTS 1 0
SALMON 0

Homerun! Grand slam! The Sprouts took the lead. With one swing of the bat, J.J. made the score 4-0.

"Irresponsible," Zoë muttered, mad at herself.

She didn't stop scratching though. None of the Salmon players did. So for the rest of the inning, they watched hits fly high and balls bounce by. It was an old-fashioned sports smackdown on the baseball battlefield.

When it ended, the heroes and their teammates plodded slowly to the dugout. They walked with their heads down and their tails between their legs.

All of them had given up hope. It looked as if the Sprouts would win the Little League championship game.

CHAPTER 9:
X-TREME BABY POWDER

Back in the dugout, the Salmon players collapsed onto their bench. Some of them grumbled. Some of them groaned. None could believe they were losing this badly.

Ten to zero! That was a football score. Abigail, for one, wasn't supposed to lose like that. She could normally carry a team to victory by herself.

"Maybe I should have eaten S.U.P.E.R. baby formula* for breakfast," she said. "Eating it always gives Zoë extra power."

*See Heroes A²Z #7: Guitar Rocket Star

Andrew was spinning in circles, trying to scratch the itches in his hard-to-reach places. When he heard Abigail, he froze.

"Three-sixty!" he exclaimed. "That's it! But we don't need power. We need powder. Baby powder. Zoë, quick, what's in your diaper?"

His baby sister blinked and blushed. "Impolite," she snapped.

"How about both?" Manager Mom interjected. "Power and powder. Just like my baby girl." Then she pulled a squeeze bottle from her purse. Its label read:

XBP X-Treme Baby Powder
Cures any rash with just one dash!

Puff! Manager Mom squeezed the bottle, and a cloud of powder filled the air.

"Quick, everyone," she said. "Run through the powder. Dash, just like the bottle says."

Naturally Abigail went first. She ignored her itchiness, cruised into the cloud, and disappeared.

After that, Manager Mom took aim. She squeezed the bottle a second time, and squeezed her eyes shut even tighter. Would her plan work? For the sake of the team, she hoped so. The championship game was on the line.

Bull's-eye! *Puff!* Another dose of powder mixed with the first. A moment later Abigail burst from the other side of the cloud.

"Score!" she cheered. "I'm cured. No more itches! Just like Zoë's ... um ... never mind!" Looking at Zoë, she changed what she was going to say in mid-thought. "Thanks, Mom!"

"Irksome," Zoë said, squinting dangerously at her sister. She wouldn't tolerate any more diaper jokes. Abigail had better never mind.

Andrew plowed into the power next. Rabbit raced, Princess pranced, and then their teammates trotted through. In seconds, everyone was itch-free. They also smelled as fresh as a spring morning.

"Here comes a homerun," Abigail said, dashing out of the dugout with a bat in her hand. She was eager to hit and score some runs. But she was also eager to get away from Zoë.

That baby could stare!

Once, Zoë had accidentally sliced the family television in half. She had been watching a spooky show and let the lasers leak out of her eyes. *Z-z-zap!* No more Knightscares for her.

No more nightmare for the Salmon today. Abigail would see to that. The only spookiness today would be the wailing of the Garden City Sprouts after they lost the game.

"Better back up," Abigail said when she came to the plate.

The Sprouts pitcher licked his green lips with his even greener tongue.

"Better plant your feet," he replied, winding up to throw. "You're about to take root."

The pitcher reared back and threw, and Abigail
tensed. This was it. The chance to rally her team. It
was time to start a comeback.

Bam! She slammed the ball with a mighty
swing. Then the strangest thing happened.

The ball exploded into a thousand tiny pieces.

CHAPTER 10:
A SPROUTING SURPRISE

"Huh?" Abigail gasped, dropping her bat. The ball had exploded. Check out that swing! Was she supposed to run to first base or just run away?

"Start your engine!" Andrew shouted from the dugout. "Get rolling!"

"Ignition!" Zoë added.

They noticed what Abigail did not. She was watching the tiny bits of baseball as they drifted down like confetti. Her siblings, on the other hand, saw them land.

The bits weren't bits. They were seeds. When they hit the ground, they sprouted and grew. Vines sprang to life like clowns launched out of jacks-in-the-box.

"Abigail, look out!" Mom shrieked.

"Run!" Dad howled.

They were back to being just parents, and the baseball game was over. Doc Bot wasn't here to play for the championship. He had a more sinister game plan.

It was so obvious. They should have seen it sooner. The Sprouts players even looked like plants. Talk about leaving clues at the scene of the crime. The Sprouts were *leaf*ing clues. Ivy leaves in their hair!

"Imposters!" Zoë growled.

Knowing this didn't help now. Abigail tried to run. Her teammates tried to reach her. But all of them were too slow. Doc Bot and his plants had surprise on their side.

"It's got me!" Abigail cried. "Mom, Dad—help!"

"We're coming!" Dad called.

"Hold on, honey!" Mom howled.

Holding on wasn't exactly what Abigail was missing. Vines and other plants wiggled, waved, and wrapped 'round her ankles. They held on tight and wouldn't let go.

No one escaped. The plants attacked from everywhere. They thrashed and lashed like the arms of angry octopi. They trapped and wrapped around arms, legs, and laps. Soon everyone was tied and bound, even the fans sitting in the grandstands.

From a distance, Comerica Park looked like a wild, overgrown potted plant.

Before the heroes could catch their breath, Doc Bot appeared out of the vegetation like a jungle cat.

"Too easy," he sneered. "The famous Heroes A²Z should have been more difficult to capture."

Abigail glared at him. "Cheater! Liar! You don't play by the rules."

"Liar?" Doc Bot laughed. "There's no lying in baseball. I play to win, and I played you. I win." He turned to J.J. at his side. "Clone them. Copy their powers."

J.J. rubbed his green hands together. "Yes, master," he said eagerly.

CHAPTER 11:
THE VEGGIE VILLAINS

Clones! That explained everything. J.J. and his teammates had green skin and ivy leaves in their hair because they were clones. Plant clones. They were Ivy League All-Stars!

And now Doc Bot was going to clone the heroes. That had been his plan the whole time. He wanted to clone the heroes and take their powers. Just like he had done to their cousin J.J.

Andrew and his sisters struggled, but they couldn't break free. Vines pinned their arms to their sides. Roots lashed their feet to the ground.

"Immobilized," Zoë snarled, but the situation only got worse.

Oversized flower petals bent down and closed over their heads like helmets. The scene looked like something out of an old horror movie. Abigail could imagine the movie villain's voice: "Behold! The human's brain will be transferred to this chicken."

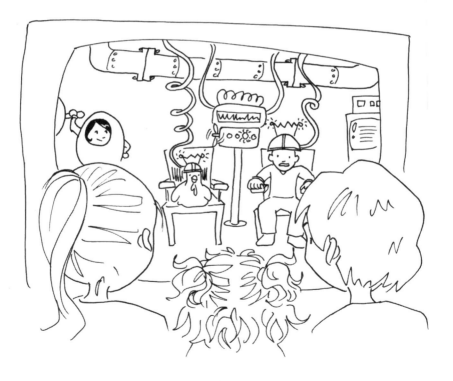

Not that the heroes had to worry about chick-ens. Not anymore at least.* Today plants were the problem. Today their powers were being planted.

Seeds sprouted in front of them, one for each hero. They quickly grew larger and morphed into pods. Whatever was inside was about to burst out.

*See Heroes A²Z #6: Fowl Mouthwash

The pod in front of Abigail burst open first. To the sporty superhero, even being cloned was a race.

Pop!

Out of the pod leaped a veggie clone. It didn't look exactly like Abigail, but it had her powers. It also had a rotten attitude.

Look out, Detroit. Here comes Abby Asparagus!

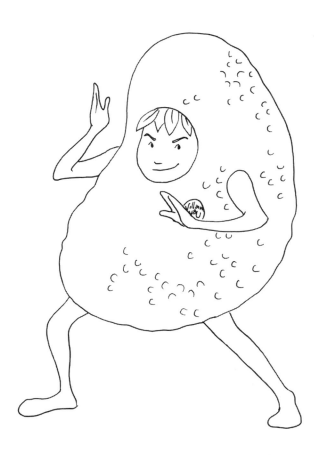

Pop! Andrew's clone popped out of its pod next. Sure, it looked kind of like him, but green wasn't exactly his color.

Ready or not, Andy Avocado was on the loose.

P-POP!

Zoë's pod burst third. It also popped the loudest.

The clone roared, flexing its green muscles. Zoey Zucchini had stomped onto the scene. Now she was ready to just stomp.

"Go, my veggie villains!" Doc Bot shouted from his blimp. "Harvest the city. Destroy Detroit!"

He cackled madly, and his cloned villains went on a rampage. They tore off in three different directions with green fire in their eyes.

Michigan, beware!

CHAPTER 12:
DESTROYING DETROIT

The vegetable villains spread out and attacked. Being the sporty super villain, Abby Asparagus stole out of the stadium first. She forced her way into Ford Field, where the Detroit Lions play football. A secret weapon awaited her there.

Footballs.

Sometimes the quarterback of a football team throws very long passes. Those passes are nicknamed "bombs."

Abby Asparagus launched dozens of bombs all over Detroit. Her pinpoint passing pounded and pummeled the city.

Zoey Zucchini secured a secret weapon next. She jetted to Jefferson Avenue and scooped up the sculpture of Joe Louis's fist. What was that? Just like it sounds. It's a twenty-four-foot long sculpture of a fist and arm. The sculpture is a tribute to legendary boxer Joe Louis, who did much for his sport but more for equality.

Zoey Zucchini, however, ignored all that. She was a villain, and villains use the good for bad. So she snatched the sculpture and clutched it like a battering ram.

Her first target? Joe Louis Arena, where the Detroit Red Wings played hockey.

Wham!   Wham!

Two quick blows from the fist brought down the walls. Just like that, with a one-two punch, Hockeytown became Sockytown.

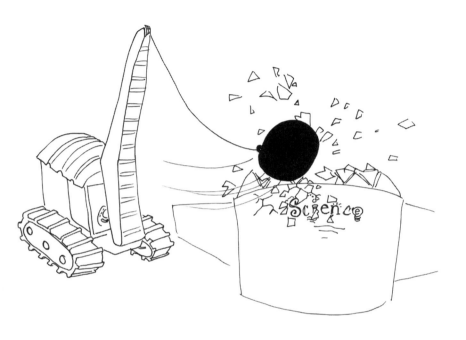

Andy Avocado found his secret weapon at a construction site. Like Andrew, he could ride anything with wheels. That included a crane with a 5,000-pound wrecking ball on its arm.

CRASH!

The glass exterior of the Detroit Science Center exploded in a sparkling shower.

If someone didn't stop Andy Avocado, Abby Asparagus, and Zoey Zucchini soon, there would be nothing left of Detroit.

CHAPTER 13:
CAPTURE THE CLONE

Ka-Boom! Smash! Crash!

Sounds of destruction echoed throughout the Motor City. They boomed over Belle Isle, tolled down Trumble Avenue, and howled through Hart Plaza. They even clanged in Comerica Park.

Cousin Clone raised a green hand to his ear. He wasn't J.J., the heroes' real cousin. The heroes knew that now.

"Do you hear that?" he asked. "The city is being destroyed. You cannot stop the Veggie Villains."

Zoë shook her head like a toddler refusing to eat. "Inferior," she said.

Cousin Clone turned his head sharply. "What did you say?" he demanded.

Zoë did her best to stay calm. Her plan was already working.

"Imitation," she shrugged. To her it was simple. Cousin Clone and the Veggie Villains were copies. They would never be as good as the originals.

Her brother caught on to this immediately. "She's right," he agreed, scanning the ball field. "The real J.J. can juggle anything. Even those baseball bats over there."

Before he finished speaking, Cousin Clone snatched the bats. There were five of them.

"These?" he sneered, tossing them into the air and starting to juggle. "Too easy. Give me a real challenge."

"Okay, fine," Abigail jumped in. "How about our gloves? Can you juggle those, too? J.J. could."

Cousin Clone rolled his eyes. One by one, he kicked the heroes' gloves into the air and added them to the bats whirling over his head.

"Not bad for an imitation?" he smirked. "Got anything else?"

The heroes shared a secret look. This was it, the daring part of their plan.

"What about us?" Andrew asked. "Think you can juggle five bats, three gloves, and three kids?"

"J.J. could," Abigail repeated.

Snap!

J.J.'s clone accepted the challenge in a snap—and with one, too. He snapped his fingers, and the vines around the heroes unraveled. The roots released their feet.

"This will prove I am as good as your cousin," the clone said. "This—"

He didn't finish. Zoë interrupted.

"Independence!" she cried. She and her siblings were free. Their plan had worked, and the plants had let go. She grabbed Abigail and Andrew by their collars and leaped into the air.

"Wilt them!" Cousin Clone bellowed.

Plants throughout the stadium came to life. Flowers fidgeted, stems swayed, bulbs burst, and roots writhed. All of them tried to hogtie the heroes.

"Hurry!" Abigail screamed. The plants were closing in.

"Fly faster!" Andrew added.

But Zoë did neither. She stopped in mid-flight, spun around, and let loose with her superbreath.

Whoosh! Gusts of wind blasted Cousin Clone, his plants, and his Garden City teammates. Back they flew, helpless. Vines entwined, and leaves weaved. Everything became a tangle.

"Beaten by baby's breath," Cousin Clone sighed, wrapped up tight.

Zoë nodded before flying free. "Incarcerated."

CHAPTER 14:
A TRIO OF TIES

"Put us down," Abigail asked her sister.

Sure, Zoë was super strong and could fly. That didn't mean she should carry Abigail and Andrew around like dolls. It was Zoë who was the baby of the trio, not the twins.

She landed outside Comerica Park and set her siblings down. Three trails of destruction led away in three different directions. The Veggie Villains had been here and gone. There was also no sign of Doc Bot or the *Dread Zeppelin.*

"Guess we have to split up," Abigail said.

The other two heroes nodded and started to run. It was time to pull some weeds.

Abigail caught her clone first. Caught it passing, that is. Abby Asparagus launched a football
bomb as Abigail rounded a corner.

Boom!

An unlucky family watching the news caught
something, too. They caught their house exploding
on TV!

Hi, Mom! We're famous!

Later, the heroes would rebuild the family's house. Right now, Abigail had to dice a vegetable.

"Game over, Asparagus," she called out. "Your time is up."

Abby Asparagus spun around and smirked. "Wrong!" she cackled. "I have your powers. I can't be beat."

An epic battle followed. Abigail and Abby Asparagus drew fencing swords from their duffel bags. They circled each other briefly and then attacked.

Clang, clang! Ting, ching!

Swords slashed. Powers clashed. The battle echoed up and down Interstate 75.

Abigail gained an early advantage. She struck and ducked, combining offense with defense. She fought forward and forced her foe back.

Abby Asparagus barely blocked and knocked those attacks aside. She gave up ground, but she didn't give up on victory.

Cling! Tang! Ching!

The two were too evenly matched. The villain and hero fought for hours, but their duel ended in a stalemate.

So did Andrew's altercation with Andy Avocado. The pair squared off in an old-fashioned demolition derby. If it had wheels, they could ride it.

Smash! Crash! Bash!

Bumper-to-bumper and nose-to-nose, they rammed and slammed until their tires fell off. In the end, however, neither driver claimed victory.

The same went for Baby Zoë and Zoey Zucchini. There was no clear winner. The tiny pair rumbled and tumbled even through the streets of Greektown.

"Invincible!" Zoey Zucchini shouted.

"Impenetrable!" Zoë countered.

Not even their eye lasers could decide a winner. Would the Heroes A^2Z and the Veggie Villains battle forever?

CHAPTER 15:
WEAKNESS FOR THE WIN

The battles could have gone on for hours, maybe days or even weeks. Heroes versus villains. Humans versus veggies. Maybe no winners would ever be crowned.

But Abigail, Andrew, and Baby Zoë couldn't allow that. Doc Bot would escape and go free.

The question was, how could the heroes win? How could they beat villains who had the exact same superpowers they had? It was like playing tug-of-war against yourself.

The Veggie Villains had the same powers as the heroes. They had the same abilities. They had the same strengths and the same—

Weaknesses.

Abigail smacked her forehead. That was it! Weaknesses. The Veggie Villains were clones. They had the heroes' superpowers, but they also had their weaknesses.

She immediately turned and fled. As an athlete, she had one weakness that was more dangerous to her than any other.

Booing. Abigail hated it. It weakened her and could make her give up.

Abigail bolted back to Comerica Park. The stadium was filled with fans. Let them choose a winner.

When she reached the field, the fans cheered. When Abby Asparagus arrived, the cheering stopped. The whole stadium went silent. Then one child yelled.

"You stink!"

After that the crowd erupted. Together they hissed one long, unbroken word.

Booooooooo!

Abby Asparagus covered her ears with her hands. "What a crowd! What a crowd!" she cried. Then she wilted like a thirsty plant, dried up, and turned to dust.

Abigail had finally won!

Yes, she had won, but there was no time to celebrate. She pumped her fist in the air once and then started to run. She had to tell her brother and sister how to defeat the other Veggie Villains.

She found Baby Zoë battling Zoey Zucchini over the Ambassador Bridge. That is the bridge that crosses the Detroit River into Canada. Lasers streaked through the air like missiles.

"Who wants to stay up late?" Abigail shouted. "Who wants to eat dessert before dinner?"

Zoë and her clone stopped fighting immedi-ately. Stay up late? Dessert before dinner? Sounded great!

"I," they both said, raising their hands.

Abigail shook her head. In a firm, clear voice, she said the word every toddler hated to hear.

"No."

Baby Zoë and Zoey Zucchini frowned. How dare Abigail tell them no! Toddlers always expected to get what they wanted. Either that or they threw tantrums.

Which is what Abigail wanted. Toddler tantrums. She grabbed a tennis ball from her duffel bag. "Ball?" she offered, tossing it playfully between her hands.

Zoë and Zucchini reached for it. A new ball—what fun!

Abigail shook her head again. "No," she repeated.

The toddlers' frowns deepened, and the pair started to sniffle. Abigail's plan was working.

"No flying in the house," she said. "No zapping vegetables.* No fighting crime after bedtime. No, no, no."

*See Heroes A²Z #1: Alien Ice Cream

On Abigail's final "no," the toddlers started to sob. Too much, too much. Stop! *Waaaaah!*

For a big finish, Abigail pretended to offer the tennis ball to Zoey Zucchini again. The toddler reached, but Abigail stuck out her tongue. She handed the ball to her sister instead.

"Infuriating!" Zoey Zucchini screeched. Her face darkened to purple. She sucked in a breath. A super-sized tantrum was about to begin.

Boom!

Too super, in fact, because she couldn't hold any more air. Zoey Zucchini exploded into tiny bits like dandelion seeds.

That left only one Veggie Villain. Andy Avocado. Abigail and Zoë knew how to take care of
him. They knew his weakness, too.

"Indianapolis," Zoë said, as in the Indianapolis 500, a 500-mile car race held every Memorial Day.

Abigail nodded. In the spirit of their brother,
she said, "Let's roll."

And roll they did. 'Round and 'round the
Motor City until they found Andrew and Andy Avo-
cado. The pair was trekking on the tracks of the
Detroit People Mover. But they weren't on the train.
They were riding scooters on its tracks!

Even so, getting their attention was easy. Zoë waved a checkered flag. To the boys, that could mean only one thing.

Time to race.

But while Zoë got them started, Abigail fixed the end. She secretly scattered darts under Andy Avocado's tires. *Pop, pop, pop!* The race ended as soon as it began. Andy Avocado's tires sagged like wilted plants.

"I've never lost before," he hissed, embarrassed. Then he deflated like his tires until—*pop!*— he disappeared. The humiliation of losing a race was more than he could take.

CHAPTER 16:
RUMBLE ON THE ROOF

"Two down," Abigail said. "One to go."

She and her siblings had defeated the clones of the Garden City Sprouts baseball team. They had also beaten the Veggie Villains. One, two. Now it was time to challenge Doc Bot.

Zoë flew to the top of the middle skyscraper of the Renaissance Center, the tallest building in Detroit. On its roof she planted a Heroes A²Z flag.

"Inalienable," she shouted at the sky. Detroit was under the heroes' protection. They would not give it up without a fight.

Doc Bot responded quickly. He rammed the *Dread Zeppelin* into high gear and descended upon the heroes. Long cannons that resembled flower petals tilted down and took aim.

"We've got your back, Zoë," Andrew said. He and Abigail had reached the roof. They wouldn't let Zoë face Doc Bot alone.

"Indebted," Zoë said to them, smiling. She meant *thank you*.

Doc Bot sneered at the heroes. "How sweet," he taunted over a loudspeaker. "Three ducks all in a row. Which is what you should do. Duck!"

Then he opened fire.

Floom! Floom! Floom! Floom! Seeds the size of softballs burst from the cannons on his blimp.

"Incoming!" Zoë yelled.

Abigail didn't listen to Doc Bot's advice. She didn't duck, dodge, or dive. She dug into her duffel bag and brought out a baseball bat.

"Doubleheader!" she cried. "Doc Bot wants to play more ball."

Pow! She plowed Doc Bot's attacking seeds deep into the Detroit River. Next stop, Canada.

"Foul!" Doc Bot screeched. "Let's see if you can hit my curve ball."

Floom! He shot again. "And my slider!" *Floom-floom!*

Suddenly seeds started spitting from his cannons faster than Abigail could swing. Zoë pitched in, firing her lasers. But the seeds came too fast. One struck the building. Then another. Then even more after that.

"Timber!" Doc Bot howled. The Renaissance Center had taken too much damage and was going to collapse.

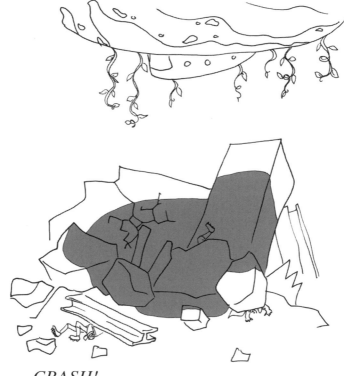

CRASH!

The Renaissance Center was made up of seven buildings, three of them skyscrapers. The tallest one fell first.

SMASH! BASH! The outer skyscrapers fell shortly after.

The heroes fell together, too. Not even Zoë's flying power could save them. The collapse was such a surprise that the heroes tumbled down helplessly along with the massive building. They hit the ground and didn't move.

High above, Doc Bot howled in triumph.

CHAPTER 17:
HOT DOG HELP

Zoë blinked slowly. What a fall! The Renaissance Center lay in ruins. She sprawled on the rubble. Her brother and sister peeked out from beneath it.

"Injuries?" she asked.

Andrew struggled to his feet. "I'm ready to roll," he replied.

"Me, too," said Abigail. "I can still play. But we need to draft another teammate or this game is over."

Zoë and Andrew glanced at their sister. Another teammate? That could mean only—

"We have to rescue J.J.," Abigail explained. "Doc Bot cloned him, so the real J.J. must be held captive somewhere."

"Imprisoned!" Zoë gasped, catching on.

Andrew nodded and quickly found some wheels. J.J. was probably in one of two places. Home or the hotel. It was Andrew's job to get his sisters there fast.

"Hop in and hold on," he said, hoping to avoid any jokes and teasing from his sisters. The closest thing with wheels, you see, was a hot dog cart.

As Andrew expected, Abigail couldn't resist.

"I sure hope Doc Bot doesn't ketchup to us," she giggled. "I don't relish the thought."

Andrew groaned. Ketchup, relish—very funny.

"Just get your buns in the cart," he replied. Hah, buns! Take that, hot dog fan.

Zoë poked them in the ribs. "Insufferable," she muttered. Doc Bot remained free. This wasn't the time for jokes.

Glumly, the twins agreed, and soon Andrew had them streaking through the streets of Detroit. A hot dog cart had never flown faster.

"There's the hotel," Abigail said, pointing ahead. "Zoë, use your x-ray vision to find J.J."

Asking was unnecessary. Zoë was already squinting at the building.

"Identified," she said after a quick scan. She spotted the real J.J. tied up on the third floor.

Unfortunately Abigail also spotted something else. The sinister shape of the *Dread Zeppelin* overhead. Doc Bot had found the heroes and was closing in again.

"Hurry, Zoë!" Abigail shouted. "Save J.J. Andrew and I will hold off Doc Bot."

Floom! Floom!

As soon as she finished speaking, Doc Bot started shooting. Abigail reached for her baseball but, but Doc Bot was faster. *Thwack!* A precise shot knocked the duffel bag out of Abigail's reach, and then vines coiled around her ankles, dragging her into the air. No homerun heroics would save her this time.

Neither would Andrew's wheeled wizardry. Rolling head over heels, he somersaulted toward Abigail's bag. Andrew wasn't a sports superstar like his sister, but he had fairly earned his spot on the Salmon team. He had hit a heap of homers in his history.

Doc Bot, however, was ready for him. The vines on his blimp lashed out and snared Andrew like a calf at a rodeo. He quickly joined his sister in the air.

Doc Bot laughed to himself. How simple! Two heroes up, two heroes down. Once he found Baby Zoë, he would make it three-for-three.

Soon the heroes would be his ... again.

CHAPTER 18:
THE SHOT HEARD 'ROUND DETROIT

Doc Bot's voice boomed over a loudspeaker. "Surrender, Baby Zoë," he demanded. "I have your siblings. You cannot win."

Slowly his words echoed into silence. Seconds passed. Then Zoë and her cousin J.J. made all kinds of noise.

Crash! With Zoë leading, the pair burst through the roof of the hotel. Once again Zoë would make her stand against Doc Bot high above the ground.

Floom! Floom-floom! Floom!

Seeds erupted from Doc Bot's cannons. They had destroyed the Renaissance Center earlier. They could flatten a hotel now.

Zoë dodged left, right, and up and down. Not one seed struck her, nor did she use her lasers to zap them.

She let J.J. catch the seeds instead. That's right. Balls, bowling pins, and blasts from a cannon—J.J. could catch and juggle them all.

Catching, after all, was an essential part of juggling. Without it, every trick would be called *the Drop. Plop, plop, plop.* Three balls on the ground. No one would pay to see that.

So J.J. could catch. Halfway there. But he could also throw, which is what he did next.

"Batter up, Zoë," he said, tossing a seed gently her way.

Wiff! Strike one! Zoë swung and missed. The bedpost she had borrowed from the hotel made a clumsy bat. Her baseball skills made a clumsier batter.

"Keep your eye on the ball," J.J. suggested. Good advice, but Zoë had heard the same thing before. The result was always the same.

Wiff! Strike two. Another miss. No surprise.

"Incapable!" she snarled, nearly giving up. Zoë just couldn't hit. Keeping her eyes on the ball never helped.

So she closed them.

And swung again when J.J. tossed her a third seed.

Pow!

Zoë connected.

Fly ball! Her third swing was her first homerun. It was the shot heard 'round Detroit.

Up and up the seed sped, powered by Zoë's super strength. Had it been clobbered in Comerica Park, the seed would have soared out of the stadium.

Would have, that is, if not for Doc Bot's blimp. Zoë's blast hit the *Dread Zeppelin* head on.

BO-OOOM!

Head on quickly became a nosedive. The blimp sagged and then fell out of the sky.

"You sank my botany ship!" Doc Bot wailed as he crashed.

No one expected what happened next. The blimp hissed like a leaky balloon, losing air and shrinking fast. But not as fast as Doc Bot. He shrank, too, and started to change.

He wasn't a man anymore. He wasn't even human. Doc Bot was just a tiny plant in a pot. His reign of green gloom was over.

"Hey!" J.J. exclaimed. "That plant was part of my school science project. I fed it some of Zoë's super-powered baby formula. I guess I fed it too much."

The other heroes agreed. That plant had caused a lot of trouble. Detroit was a mess! Someone had to clean up the city.

"Impersonators?" Zoë suggested. The Garden City Sprouts clones could repair and rebuild the city. They could do something good before they wilted.

As for the real Sprouts players, the heroes rescued them with J.J.'s help. Soon they were free and on the baseball field in Comerica Park.

"Play ball!" the umpire shouted. The real championship game was about to begin.

Abigail pitched. J.J. hit. A long fly ball streaked toward the outfield fence …

Abigail, Andrew, and Baby Zoë played hard. They wanted to win the championship. But they also remembered that baseball was a game. Winning wasn't as important as keeping America safe. Danger had found them on the ball field. It could also surprise them on a family vacation to beautiful Mackinac Island in …

Book #10:
Joey Down Under

www.realheroesread.com

Visit the Website

realheroesread.com

Watch Heroes A2Z Mini-Movies
Meet Authors Charlie & David
Read Sample Chapters
See Fan Artwork
Join the Free Fan Club
Invite Charlie & David to Your School
Lots More!

Fighting Crime Before Bedtime

... and more!

Visit
www.realheroesread.com
for the latest news

#1: Cauldron Cooker's Night

David Anthony
Charles David

#2: Skull in the Birdcage

#3: Early Winter's Orb

#4: Voyage to Silvermight
The Dragonsbane Horn Book One

David Anthony
Charles David

#5: Trek Through Tanglewood
The Dragonsbane Horn Book Two

#6: Hunt the Hallowdeep
The Dragonsbane Horn Book Three

David Anthony
Charles David

#7: The Ninespire Experiment

David Anthony
Charles David

#8: Aware of the Wolf

Also by David Anthony and Charles David

Knightscares

Monsters. Magic. Mystery.

Visit
www.realheroesread.com
to learn more

Learn to Juggle
with J.J.

Hi, everyone! J.J. here. I'm going to teach you how to juggle in three easy steps. Get yourself three balls. Juggling balls work best, but you can use golf balls or rolled up socks. Just don't use eggs or Christmas ornaments.

Step 1

Start with one ball. Toss it from your right hand to your left in an arc about eye level. Then toss it back to your right in a similar arc. Practice this until you can catch the ball every time wthout looking at your hands. Keep your eye on the ball.

Step 2

Once you've mastered Step 1, pick up another ball. You're ready for two. Hold a ball in each hand. Toss the ball in your right to your left hand. When it reaches mid-arc, toss the ball in your left hand to your right. Be sure to toss the 2nd ball in a similar arc. Do not hand the ball off to your right hand. That would be passing with style, not juggling. Both balls must arc up near your eyes. Don't rush it.

Step 3

After you can juggle two balls, juggling three is not as hard as you might think. You can do it! Hold two balls in your right hand. Hold one in your left. First, toss one ball from your right hand to left. When it reaches mid-arc, toss the ball in your left hand to your right. Finally, toss the third ball when your second throw reaches mid-arc. Repeat this for as long as you can. You're juggling!

Visit the website realheroesread.com to watch the author Charles David Clasman juggle. He demonstrates these three steps in a video online. Check it out! Real heroes read!

realheroesread.com

Connect with the Authors

Charlie:
charlie@sigilpublishing.com
facebook.com/charlesdavidclasman
twitter.com/charliedclasman

David:
david@sigilpublishing.com
facebook.com/authordavidanthony
twitter.com/authordavid

Visit the Website

REAL
HEROES
READ!

realheroesread.com

Sigil Publishing, LLC

P.O. Box 824
Leland, MI 49654

Email:
info@sigilpublishing.com

About the Illustrator
Lys Blakeslee

Lys graduated from Grand Valley State University in Michigan where she earned a degree in Illustration.

She has always loved to read, and devoted much of her childhood to devouring piles of books from the library.

She lives in Wyoming, MI with her wonderful parents, two goofy cats, and one extra-loud parakeet.

Thank you, Lys!